BONE SOUP

For Bill, who makes every Halloween
a bone-chilling treat,
and for Paula, a piff-poof magical editor!
—A. S. C.

For Ant, Charlotte, and Betty Jones,
who always share their soup.
—T. K.

SIMON & SCHUSTER BOOKS FOR YOUNG READERS
An imprint of Simon & Schuster Children's Publishing Division
1230 Avenue of the Americas, New York, New York 10020

Book design by Chloë Foglia • The text for this book was set in Caslon.
The illustrations for this book were rendered using charcoal and pencils, and colored digitally.
Manufactured in China • 0518 SCP
First Edition
2 4 6 8 10 9 7 5 3 1
CIP data for this title is available from the Library of Congress.
ISBN 978-1-4814-8608-8 (hardcover)
ISBN 978-1-4814-8609-5 (eBook)

BONE SOUP

A SPOOKY, TASTY TALE

Alyssa Satin Capucilli

Illustrated by Tom Knight

A PAULA WISEMAN BOOK
Simon & Schuster Books for Young Readers
New York London Toronto Sydney New Delhi

One Halloween morning, three very hungry witches were looking for a tasty treat. They checked the cupboards only to find nothing there.

"Bare," said Naggy Witch.
"Empty," said Craggy Witch.
"Only a small, dry bone," said Scraggy Witch. "Only a bone."

"Let's make bone soup, sisters," cackled Naggy Witch gleefully.
"Bone soup is the perfect Halloween treat."

The three witches
carried their cauldron and bone far and away until
they came to a door. The witches hadn't even begun to knock
when . . . the door groaned open. And there, the scariest looking
monster they had ever seen towered before them! It made the
witches shiver. But, alas, they were very hungry!

"Trick-or-treat! Trick-or-treat!
We've something unusually good to eat.
It's bone soup, soup from a bone,"
said Naggy Witch.

"Bone soup?
Impossible!
Go away!
There will be time
for your tricks later,"
boomed the monster.

"PIFF-POOF!
It's no trick.
A bit of water is all we need,"
promised Naggy Witch.

"I'm hungry, Papa,"
said a little monster as she appeared at the door.
"Can we make bone soup, please?"
"None of your tricks?" boomed the monster.
"Piff-poof! Only a treat," Naggy Witch replied.
And in minutes, the bone and the water
were bubbling inside the cauldron.

Naggy Witch gave the cauldron a stir.
She took a small taste.

"Bewitching," she said. "If only we had something savory!
That's all it needs. But where can we find it?"
"Look! Another door!" said Craggy Witch.

The three witches hadn't even begun to knock when . . . the door opened with a hiss! And there, the spookiest ghost they had ever seen floated before them! It made the witches tremble, but, alas, they were very hungry.

And as the ghost was feeling a bit hungry, a most savory eye of a giant was soon bubbling in the cauldron.

"Bedazzling," said Naggy Witch after a small taste.
"If only we had something . . . crunchy!"
And with that, the eeriest of ghouls brought forth
a long, crackly lizard's tail!

"PIFF-POOF!
Into the cauldron it goes!"
cried Naggy Witch.

An unusual scent began to waft through the air now.
Doors creaked open; windows squeaked wide too.
“Beguiling,” said Naggy Witch. “But I wonder: Can a
tasty tidbit or two be found?”

"Juice of a toad, earthworms, dried dragon wings,"
drooled a bat.
"Colored flies, hot and sweet,"
snarled a goblin.
"Sludge; slimy sludge,"
whispered a mummy.
"Claws, claws, and more claws,"
rattled a skeleton.

"PIFF-POOF! Hypnotizing,"
murmured Naggy Witch,
mixing and stirring,
mixing and stirring.
"Wrinkled fingers,
o-o-o-old toenails,"
howled a werewolf.
"Dead leaves, cobwebs, and . . .

. . *the* wrinkliest of prunes,"

snickered a vampire.

Even Naggy Witch
had to gasp!

Now the crowd was growing hungrier and hungrier and hungrier. . . .
"Bone soup? Soup from a bone? This better not be a trick," growled the monster. He was feeling particularly fierce and quite hungry just then.

"I'll take back that eye," warned the ghost.
"And the crackly tail," grumbled the ghoul.
"I won't hang around much longer," sneered the bat.
"I'll use powers of my own," scowled the goblin.
"Let's wrap this up now," mumbled the mummy.
"Don't rattle me further," clattered the skeleton.
"O-o-o, let's go!" howled the werewolf.
"Before it's too late," snarled the vampire, baring his fangs. . . .

"BONE SOUP, SOUP FROM A BONE,"
they whispered.
"BONE SOUP, SOUP FROM A BONE!"
they chanted.

"BONE SOUP!
SOUP FROM A
BONE!"

they roared.

"Wait! I know what it needs,"
called a small voice.
"You do?" asked Naggy Witch.

"Three taps of your
wand, Scraggy Witch,"
said the little monster.

“Two spins of your broom, Craggy Witch.”

WHIRL-WHIRL

“And one wave of your cape, Naggy Witch, if you please.”

WHOO-OO-OO-SH

Naggy Witch waved her cape over the bubbling brew. Then she mixed, and she stirred, and she took one more taste . . .

SLUR-R-R-P

"Piff-Poof! Imagine that!" Naggy Witch cackled gleefully.

"Bone soup . . . and it's ready at last!"

"Trick-or-treat! Trick-or-treat!" called Naggy Witch.

"We've something unusually good to eat!"

And as a full moon rose in the sky, the three witches filled a steaming bowl of bone soup for all. It was made with ingredients tried and true, and some *monsterishly* new. The soup was scary, spooky, eerie, bewitching, bedazzling, beguiling, hypnotizing, and spellbinding . . .

. . . but most of all, piff-poof,
it was bone-chillingly delicious.

Naggy Witch's Bone Soup

Bone (A ham bone or turnip)
Water for brew (32 oz. chicken or vegetable broth)
Eye of a giant (1 onion, chopped)
Claws (1 clove garlic, chopped)
Juice of a toad (3 tablespoons olive oil)
Lizard's tail (2 stalks celery, chopped)
Wrinkled fingers (2 carrots and 2 parsnips, peeled and cut into one-inch pieces)
Dried dragon wings (½ head red or green cabbage, washed and chopped)
Colored flies (Red pepper flakes, black pepper, and salt to taste)
Green sludge (1 can stewed tomatoes)
Earthworms (1 cup fusilli pasta, cooked)
Old toenails (1 can cannellini beans, rinsed and drained)
Dead leaves (Small bunch of kale, chopped)
Wrinkly prune (If you dare . . . gasp! Or add 1 sundried tomato!)
Cobwebs (¼ cup shredded parmesan cheese)

- With a parent or caring adult, gather your ingredients and utensils.
- In a large cauldron or pot, brew water and bone over a medium flame. With a gleeful cackle, say, "Piff-poof," aloud.
- Add the eye of a giant, claws, and juice of a toad. Repeat, "Piff-poof!" Mix and stir.
- Drop in the lizard's tail, wrinkled fingers, dried dragon wings. Add the colored flies. Mix and stir.
- Pour in the sludge. "Piff-poof!"
- When brew begins to boil, add the earthworms.
- Stir in old toenails, dead leaves, and a wrinkly prune.
- Cook about 20 minutes.
- Add 3 taps of a wand, 2 spins of a broom, and 1 wave of a cape.
- Sprinkle with cobwebs, wait for a full moon, and with a howling "Piff-poof!" . . . serve the treat to all!

A note from the author on *Stone Soup* and *Bone Soup*

Stone Soup is a very old folktale that has been told repeatedly over time and, amazingly, all across the world. While each version may vary from the next, *Stone Soup* is a tale of making something from nothing. The best stone soup is made when characters work together, pool their resources, and contribute whatever they can to share with others. Sometimes there is a trickster or a beggar who is seeking food he or she has been denied. Still, I like to focus on the aspect of small gifts of good things coming together to benefit all. Rather than a trick, we have a most tasty treat! The ingredients needed for stone soup, or in this case, bone soup, are similar to a recipe for creating a story. We put in a little of this and a little of that, we mix and we stir and we taste, sometimes over and over again, until it is just right . . . of course, we do try to add a bit of magic, too! And sharing the story? Well, that is the best part of all.

Naggy Witch's Bone Soup

Bone	(A ham bone or turnip)
Water for brew	(32 oz. chicken or vegetable broth)
Eye of a giant	(1 onion, chopped)
Claws	(1 clove garlic, chopped)
Juice of a toad	(3 tablespoons olive oil)
Lizard's tail	(2 stalks celery, chopped)
Wrinkled fingers	(2 carrots and 2 parsnips, peeled and cut into one-inch pieces)
Dried dragon wings	(½ head red or green cabbage, washed and chopped)
Colored flies	(Red pepper flakes, black pepper, and salt to taste)
Green sludge	(1 can stewed tomatoes)
Earthworms	(1 cup fusilli pasta, cooked)
Old toenails	(1 can cannellini beans, rinsed and drained)
Dead leaves	(Small bunch of kale, chopped)
Wrinkly prune	(If you dare . . . gasp! Or add 1 sundried tomato!)
Cobwebs	(¼ cup shredded parmesan cheese)

- With a parent or caring adult, gather your ingredients and utensils.
- In a large cauldron or pot, brew water and bone over a medium flame. With a gleeful cackle, say, "Piff-poof," aloud.
- Add the eye of a giant, claws, and juice of a toad. Repeat, "Piff-poof!" Mix and stir.
- Drop in the lizard's tail, wrinkled fingers, dried dragon wings. Add the colored flies. Mix and stir.
- Pour in the sludge. "Piff-poof!"
- When brew begins to boil, add the earthworms.
- Stir in old toenails, dead leaves, and a wrinkly prune.
- Cook about 20 minutes.
- Add 3 taps of a wand, 2 spins of a broom, and 1 wave of a cape.
- Sprinkle with cobwebs, wait for a full moon, and with a howling "Piff-poof!" . . . serve the treat to all!

A note from the author on *Stone Soup* and *Bone Soup*

Stone Soup is a very old folktale that has been told repeatedly over time and, amazingly, all across the world. While each version may vary from the next, *Stone Soup* is a tale of making something from nothing. The best stone soup is made when characters work together, pool their resources, and contribute whatever they can to share with others. Sometimes there is a trickster or a beggar who is seeking food he or she has been denied. Still, I like to focus on the aspect of small gifts of good things coming together to benefit all. Rather than a trick, we have a most tasty treat! The ingredients needed for stone soup, or in this case, bone soup, are similar to a recipe for creating a story. We put in a little of this and a little of that, we mix and we stir and we taste, sometimes over and over again, until it is just right . . . of course, we do try to add a bit of magic, too! And sharing the story? Well, that is the best part of all.